For Nicholas
L.J.

For Lily Mae,
welcome to the world!
C.W.

First published in 1995 by Magi Publications
55 Crowland Avenue, Hayes, Middlesex UB3 4JP

This edition published in 1995

Text © 1994 by Linda Jennings
Illustrations © 1994 by Catherine Walters

The right of Linda Jennings to be identified as the author
of this work has been asserted by her in accordance with
The Copyright, Designs and Patents Act 1988.

Printed and bound in Belgium by Proost N.V. Turnhout

ISBN 1 85430 126 8

MILLIE

by

Linda Jennings

illustrated by

Catherine Walters

Magi Publications, London

$\mathcal{M}$illie was a lop-eared rabbit who lived in a hutch.
Her brothers and sisters munched away quite happily on
their lettuce-leaves, but Millie was different.

"I want to be free," she said. But, above all, she wanted
to meet a wild rabbit.

"Don't be stupid," said Billy. "Wild rabbits are *fierce*."

"They'd eat you up," added Lily.

"They smell," said Dilly, woffling her nose.

One evening someone left the hutch door open.
This was Millie's chance! With a flick of her little white
tail she was off and away!
"Come back, Millie," called Billy, Dilly and Lily, but Millie
took no notice.
Beyond the garden lay a big field. Millie could just see it,
if she stood on her hind legs and looked through
the hedge.
"That's where the wild rabbits must live," she thought.
She burrowed underneath, and came out on the
other side . . .

. . . where a fox was waiting for her!
Millie had never seen a fox before. She stared
at him, without moving. The fox licked his lips.
He took a step forward . . .
"RUN, YOU STUPID THING, RUN!" cried a
gruff voice, and suddenly the field was filled with
rabbits, racing towards their burrows.
Millie didn't have time to think – she ran too.
"In here," ordered the same voice, and Millie
shot right down a hole at her feet.

The fox tried to follow, but could not fit through the
entrance to the burrow.

"That was a close one," said the wild rabbit. "Nearly had you,
did that old fox!" He touched Millie's nose. "You don't half
look funny," he said. "Why are your ears drooping down?"

"Because I'm a lop-eared rabbit," said Millie. She thought
the wild rabbit looked funny too, with his dull grey coat
and pricked-up ears. He wasn't fierce, though, and he had
saved her life.

When the fox had gone, the two rabbits came up into the field again.

"I'm Seventy Six," said the wild rabbit. "We're called by numbers because there are so many of us." The rabbit thought Millie was a soppy name, and said so.

"You're very rude," said Millie, trying to clean the earth off her coat.

"I speak my mind," said Seventy-Six. But he didn't tell Millie she was the prettiest rabbit he'd ever seen.

The sun was setting and the field was tinged with a rosy-pink glow. The two rabbits chased each other round and round the oak tree and all over the field.

Seventy-Six was much faster than Millie, and she was soon
panting for breath.
"I'm not used to running," she puffed. "But isn't it wonderful
to be free?"
Millie and Seventy-Six suddenly skidded to a stop.

A whole line of rabbits was sitting at the edge of the field, staring at them.

"Don't worry," said Seventy-Six. "It's only my family."

The rabbits crowded closer.

"What's *that*?" asked one.

"It's a namby-pamby tame rabbit," said another.

"We can't have funny-looking rabbits here," said Father Rabbit.

"Especially brainless rabbits who attract foxes."

"Go back to where you came from," snapped Seventy-Six's uncle.

Millie looked at the unfriendly wild rabbits and trembled.
Her brother Billy had been right. They did look very fierce,
but she was determined not to show them she was afraid.
"All right, I'll go," she said. "See if I care!"
A big buck rabbit advanced on her with bared teeth.
"Yes, push off!" he snapped. "We don't want the likes
of you here!" He thumped the ground with his powerful
back legs. Millie gave him a bold stare, turned up her little
woffly nose, and scampered back across the field.
The big buck rabbit chased her as far as the hedge.
"AND DON'T YOU DARE COME BACK AGAIN,"
he roared at her.

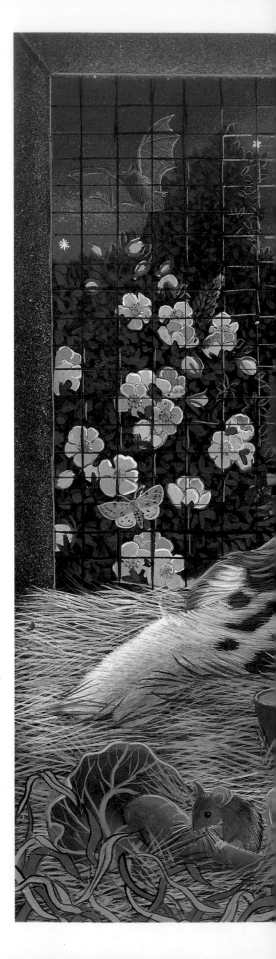

Millie dug her way back into the garden.
Her heart was still beating fast. She wondered
what had happened to Seventy-Six. She felt sad,
because she had wanted to be friends with him.

Millie hopped back to the hutch, but the door
was now locked, and Billy, Dilly and Lily fast
asleep. She began to nibble at the wire, but then
stopped. The hutch looked very small and dark.
She remembered how miserable she had been
living in it.

Millie hopped down the garden again. It looked
quite different in the dark. Shadows moved in
the bushes. A cat yeowled. Something small
scuttled down the path – and something
larger was coming across the lawn towards her.
Was it the fox? Millie was tired of being chased,
but as she turned tail to run back to the hutch,
a familiar sounding voice called out to her . . .

"Millie, it's me – Seventy-Six! I told them if they didn't want you, then I would go, too," he said. "And I did."

So Seventy-Six had come into the garden to find her!

"I don't want to live in the hutch any more," said Millie. "I want to be free, like you!"

"You don't mind living wild?" asked Seventy-Six.

"Not if we can be together," said Millie.

So Millie and Seventy-Six left the garden and the field
and travelled on to look for a new home . . .
. . . and they found one that was exactly right!

Now Millie and Seventy-Six have a very special secret . . .
And if you come with me, over the hill and into the
bluebell wood, you will see what it is!